little book **BIG**

What is art?

NoodleJUICE

Noodle Juice Ltd
www.noodle-juice.com
Stonesfield House, Stanwell Lane, Great Bourton, Oxfordshire, OX17 1QS
First published in Great Britain 2023
Copyright © Noodle Juice Ltd 2023
Text by Noodle Juice 2022 • Illustrations by Katie Rewse 2022
All rights reserved
Printed in China
A CIP catalogue record of this book is available from the British Library.
ISBN: 978-1-915613-69-1
1 3 5 7 9 10 8 6 4 2

What is art?

(page 4)

The ability to create and appreciate art is an important part of being human. But what – EXACTLY – is art? How do we know what is art and what isn't?

Let's ask some questions to see if we can work it out!

What does art do?
(page 6)

When did art start?
(page 8)

What can you make art with?
(page 10)

What is a painting?
(page 12)

What is a sculpture?
(page 14)

What is pottery?
(page 16)

What is modern art?
(page 18)

Can you use a computer
to make art?
(page 20)

How do we know if
art is any good?
(page 22)

What can you
do with art?
(page 24)

How can art
help people?
(page 26)

3

What is art?

Art is something that is made to be looked at only for pleasure. Or to spark an emotional reaction.

Art can be a painting, a sculpture, a building or a statue. It can also be a piece of pottery.

Artists make works that are beautiful or which make us think differently about things.

Here are three different ways to describe art: representation, expression and form.

REPRESENTATION
This is when the artist recreates something beautiful or meaningful from real life, such as a flower or animal.

EXPRESSION
Here the artist wants to convey a feeling or an emotion.

FORM
This kind of art is the formal arrangement of lines, colour or shapes to create an abstract impression of something.

What does art do?

Art has many different purposes.

Art can **celebrate** a person's life or achievements.

GALLERY

EXHIBITION

EXHIBITION

Art can help us appreciate other **cultures**.

Art can tell a **story**.

Art can be used to **persuade** people to think differently.

Great art should move the viewer in some way, but it can also be good for us...

Creating art ourselves allows us to share how we **feel**. Art can be a form of expression.

A lot of art is beautiful. Looking at beautiful things can give us **hope**.

Looking at art can make us stop and reflect on how we feel. That is good for our **mental health**.

Completing a painting or sculpture can make us feel good about ourselves. Art can make us feel **confident**.

When did art start?

Long ago, people lived in caves and told their stories by painting on **cave walls**.

The ancient Greeks decorated vases with black figures.

In Egypt, **statues and wall paintings** were used to decorate pharoahs' tombs.

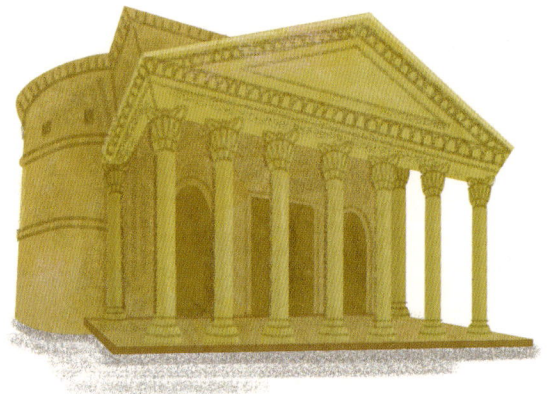

The Romans built **the Pantheon** over two thousand years ago.

During the Middle Ages, **illuminated manuscripts** and tapestries helped to tell stories.

Chinese artists used **jade and ceramics**, as well as silk, to create images of nature.

Renaissance painters, such as Leonardo da Vinci, used oil paints to create masterpieces.

Now, some artists work with **computers and cameras** to produce their work.

What can you make art with?

With **oil paints**...

With **charcoal**, pastels or crayons.

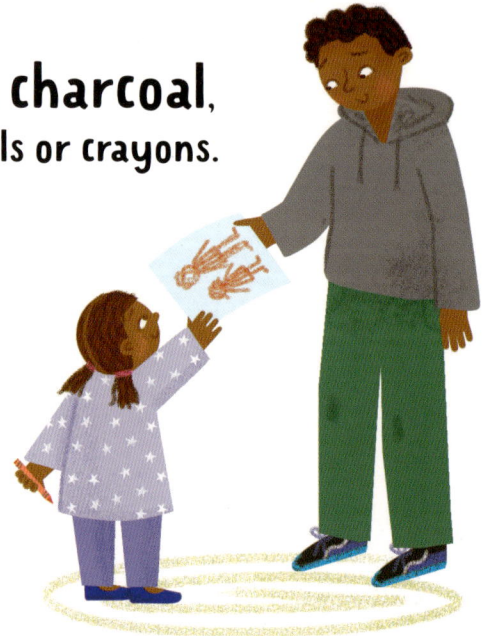

...or **watercolours**.

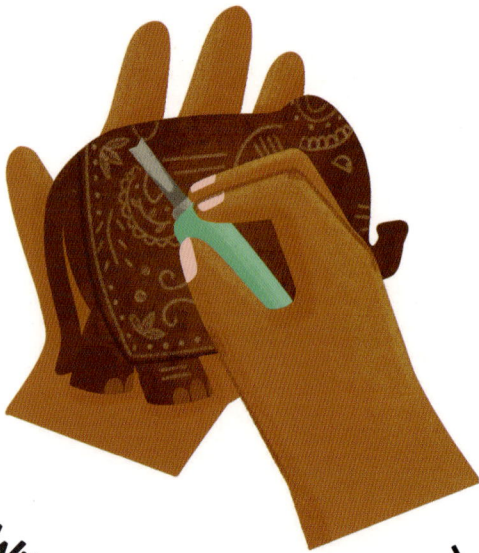

With **ceramics**.

With marble, **bronze** or wood.

With **spray paints**.

With **lights**.

Or a crumpled **bed sheet**.

Some people create body art and use ink to draw **tattoos**.

Others surround **islands** with pieces of material.

You can make art with almost **anything**.

What is a painting?

Most simply, a painting is a 2-D picture made using paint on a flat surface. The surface can be a canvas or even a ceiling.

Artists normally use a paintbrush to create their paintings, but some use their hands or feet. Others might use a bucket to throw colour across the surface.

Some paintings have an **elaborate frame**, others have no frame at all.

There have been many different styles of painting over the centuries. Here are some of the most popular.

Impressionism

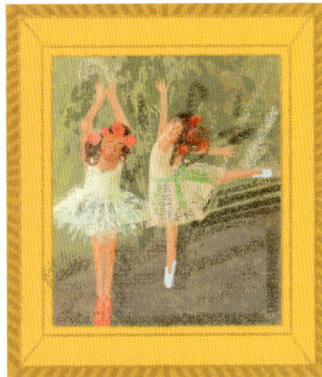

Art nouveau

Baroque

Art deco

Classicism

Renaissance art

13

What is a sculpture?

A sculpture is a 3-D model made from a variety of materials. Sculptors use stone, clay, wood or metal to create their works.

A sculpture can either be **in the round**, which means it can be seen from all sides...

...or **in relief**, which means they project out from a wall or background.

Metal sculptures are often cast by pouring **molten** metal, such as bronze, into a mould.

Some sculptors work on a **large** scale.

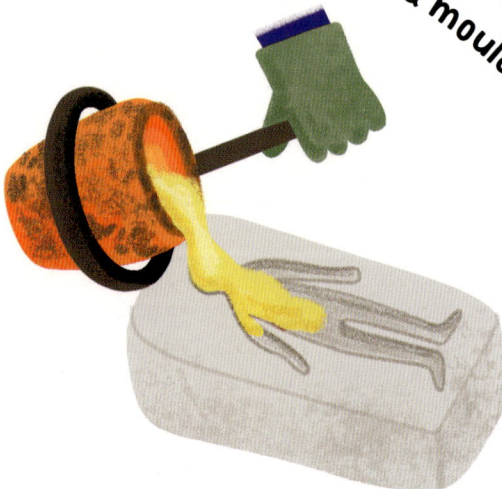

Other artists like working in **miniature**.

With some sculptures it can be more important to look at what isn't there, than what is.

What is pottery?

Pottery has been used as art for thousands of years. Artists use clay to create their work and then fire it at very high temperatures to make it hard.

A piece of art made from pottery could be a vase or a plate, or even a teapot. But it doesn't have to be useful. It can simply be nice to look at.

Potters can build their pieces by **hand**.

Or they can use a **potter's wheel**.

One of the earliest ways potters decorated their vases was by **stamping** them with a pattern.

Potters use **glazes or oxides** – metallic powders – to add colour. These effects can be surprising as the heat causes a different reaction almost every time.

Very delicate pottery is made from porcelain. Say it like this:

PAW-suh-LIN

Soapstone is added to clay and the items are fired at over 1,100°C (2,000°F).

17

What is modern art?

Modern art is used to describe artworks created towards the end of the 19th century and during the 20th and 21st centuries. These are some of the most famous modern art movements.

Pop art

Cubism

Surrealism

Futurism

Some modern artists use different materials in their work. This is called **mixed-media**. They often create set pieces, called installations, for people to view.

Other artists, called **street artists**, create art on the walls of cities and towns for all to share.

Can you use a computer to make art?

These days, you don't have to use traditional materials to create works of art. Now, artists and illustrators use digital tools to make amazing pieces. This book was illustrated using art created on a computer.

Creating images digitally takes just as much thought, skill and creativity as using a paintbrush. There are also benefits to making your art on a laptop or tablet.

You can take your art with you **wherever** you go.

You can easily fix any **mistakes**.

You can save **time** and storage space.

It is easier to work with people from all over the **world**.

There is a **digital tool** for every style you wish to draw or paint – and more are being created all the time.

How do we know if art is any good?

We like art for different reasons, but just because we like something doesn't mean that it is good. There are many things to consider.

Does the image looks like the object it is trying to represent?

Remember **different** *schools of art might represent an apple in different ways.*

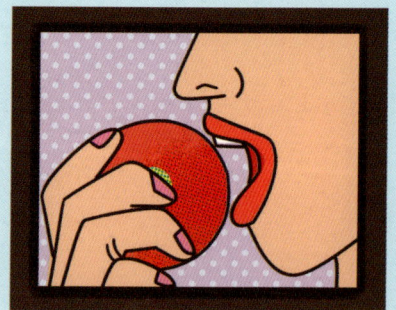

Here are some more questions to ask yourself
when you are looking at a piece of art.

What's the **history** of
the apple artwork?

Does the apple sculpture
stay in your **memory**?

Has the apple been
drawn or painted **well**?

What is the picture of the
apple trying to **tell** you?

THIS
is an
APPLE

What can you do with art?

Creating your own art can be extremely satisfying. You can display it at home or give it as a gift. But did you know that you can also use your art skills in a career? Here are some of the roles you could think about.

An illustrator creates pictures that illustrate ideas or stories.

A designer uses graphics and images to create magazines, books or even food packaging.

An art teacher helps others to learn how to paint, draw or sculpt.

A conservator helps to preserve and repair damaged artworks.

An **animator** works in film, TV and computer games and uses software to make their art move.

A **curator** works in a museum and puts together exhibitions for people to come and see.

An **artist** creates pieces to sell to individuals, businesses or galleries.

An **auctioneer** values artworks and then helps auction – or sell – them.

An **art therapist** uses art to help people overcome problems, such as anxiety or illness.

How does art help people?

Creating art allows you to explore your **emotions** and feelings.

Simply colouring a picture can **help** relieve stress and anxiety.

Making art can help people suffering from memory loss or illness, by creating more **connections** in their brains.

Working on a big art project together can strengthen a **community**.

Art is important for our society too.

It can be used to influence how we think, and promote what is good.

Art helps us to share cultures and beliefs.

It also allows us to look at the past and experience the world as it was then.

Art can take complicated ideas and make them more easily understood.

So ... do we know what art is?

We know that art is good for us individually and as a society.

We know what art IS and what it DOES.

We understand where art STARTED.

We know what you USE to make art.

We know what a painting, a sculpture and pottery are.

We know about different TYPES of painting.

We understand that COMPUTERS can be used to make art.

We know if a piece of art is GOOD, and we understand what we can DO with art.

But it is also very important that we understand what art is worth. This is about how a painting or statue can feed our imagination, not just what it would sell for.

A world without art would be a very dull place.

Why don't you think about what you would like to do with art in the future?

Glossary

Abstract art   a picture that uses shapes, texture and colour to represent a real object

Achievement   a thing done well, with effort

Appreciate   to see the value of, to be grateful for, to admire

Bronze   a yellowish-brown metal made from copper and tin

Canvas   a strong cloth made from hemp or flax used to make sails, tents and as a surface for oil paintings

Cast   to shape molten metal in a mould

Ceramic   clay that has been hardened by heat

Confident   to feel assured and certain

Elaborate   detailed and complicated in design or finish

Emotional reaction   a strongly felt response

Exhibition   a collection of things on public display

Expression   showing how you feel through art or music

Fire   to heat clay to a high temperature to harden it

Futurism   an artistic movement that celebrated technology

Graphics   images used in design

History   the study of the past

Illuminated manuscript   pages decorated by hand, from the Middle Ages

Impression   a feeling or an idea about something or someone

Influence   to have an effect on something or someone

Jade   a semi-precious green stone

Marble   a hard form of limestone with streaks or patterns

Masterpiece   an outstanding work of art

Meaningful   important, serious and worthwhile

Memory   where your brain stores and remembers information

Mental health someone's emotional well-being

Mould a hollow vessel which shapes molten metal

Original inventive and new

Persuade to make someone do something through reasoning

Pleasure a feeling of satisfaction and happiness

Pop art an artistic movement that celebrated modern culture and mass media

Pottery dishes, vessels and pots made from fired clay

Preserve to keep something in its original condition

Promote to support or encourage something

Purpose the reason to do something or for something to exist

Recreate to reproduce something

Reflect to think carefully and deeply

Renaissance a period in European history when art and literature thrived

Represent to act or speak on someone's behalf

Silk a fine, luxurious fabric made from the threads produced by silkworms

Soapstone a soft stone made from magnesium silicate

Society a community of people defined by common values

Surrealism an artistic movement that encouraged creativity by putting odd things together

Tapestry a pictorial wall hanging made by weaving or embroidering a canvas

Traditional long-established, done in a specific way

Viewer someone who looks at something

Work a piece of art, music or literature